OTHER YEARLING BOOKS
BY PATRICIA REILLY GIFF YOU WILL ENJOY:

YEARLING BOOKS/YOUNG YEARLINGS/YEARLING CLASSICS are designed especially to entertain and enlighten young people. Patricia Reilly Giff, consultant to this series, received the bachelor's degree from Marymount College. She holds the master's degree in history from St. John's University, and a Professional Diploma in Reading from Hofstra University. She was a teacher and reading consultant for many years, and is the author of numerous books for young readers.

For a complete listing of all Yearling titles, write to
Dell Readers Service, P.O. Box 1045,
South Holland, IL 60473.

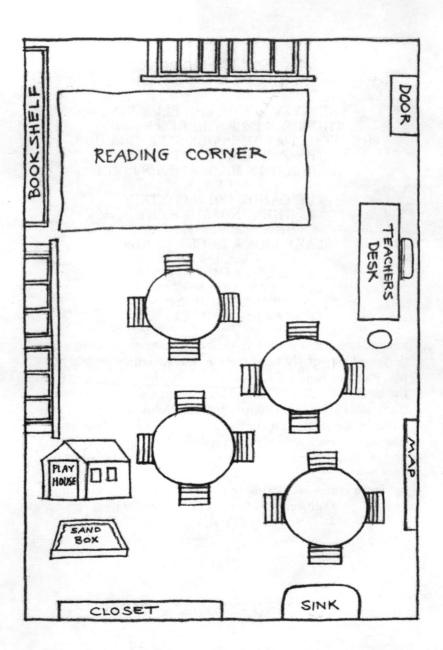

New Kids
3
at the Polk Street School

All About Stacy

Patricia Reilly Giff

Illustrated by Blanche Sims

A YOUNG YEARLING BOOK

Published by
Dell Publishing
a division of
Bantam Doubleday Dell Publishing Group, Inc.
666 Fifth Avenue
New York, New York 10103

For Sister Claudia, C.S.J.

ISBN: 0-440-40088-0

Printed in the United States of America

November 1988

10 9 8 7 6 5 4

WES

CHAPTER

1

Stacy Arrow held her face up.

A snowflake landed on her nose.

"I'm freezing," she said.

"Me too," said her best friend, Jiwon.

"We're poor little children." Stacy dug her hands in her pockets. "Out in the snow. No mother. No father. No food."

"Oh, no," said Jiwon.

"Oh, yes," said Stacy. "And we're lost too."

Just then the bell rang.

They raced to their line.

The class marched inside.

Mrs. Zachary was standing in front.

She was smiling.

"Hurry," she said. "We're going to do something exciting."

Stacy looked around.

The room was a mess.

Boxes were all over the place.

Red ones. Green ones. Striped ones.

Stacy hurried.

She put her mittens in her pocket.

She tore out of her jacket.

She raced to the closet.

In two minutes she was back.

So was everyone else.

"This is the fastest class," said Mrs. Zachary.

She sat on the edge of her desk. "Guess what?"

Stacy's hand shot up. "It's something about the boxes."

"Smart girl, Stacy," said Mrs. Zachary.

She smiled with her teeth.

They were big ones. Big and white.

They stuck out a little.

Stacy loved the way they looked.

She stuck out her own teeth and smiled.

Eddie raised his hand. "Is there something to eat in the boxes?"

Everyone laughed.

Eddie was always thinking about food.

He had the best snacks in the class.

"Sorry, Eddie." Mrs. Zachary

shook her head. "Here's what we're going to do."

She held up a box.

It was blue and yellow.

"This week, we'll make About-Me boxes."

"Yahoodie," Patty said. She jangled her red heart bracelet.

That's what she always did.

Sometimes Stacy got sick of the jangling.

She got sick of the yahoodies too.

Stacy looked over at Jiwon. She was jumping up and down.

Stacy felt like jumping up and down too.

It was going to be a great week.

"Everyone will get a box," said Mrs. Zachary.

Stacy looked hard at the boxes.

She saw just the one she wanted.

It was purple.

It was a perfect About-Me box.

"What's a Loud-Me box?" Twana asked.

Everyone laughed again.

Twana was always mixing up words.

"About Me," said Mrs. Zachary.

"Eddie will put Eddie things in his box. A.J. will put A.J. things in his."

Stacy wondered what Mrs. Zachary was talking about.

She wondered if she were going to get the purple box.

Maybe she should move her seat a little.

Edge up to the front of the room.

Get close to the purple box.

She pushed her chair with her feet.

It made a scritchy noise.

Mrs. Zachary didn't hear it. "I like cats." She held up a magazine. "I'll cut one out for my About-Me box."

"I like dogs," said Twana. "That's what I'll put in."

Stacy scritched her chair a little farther.

She headed up the aisle.

"I'll bring my baby picture," said A.J.

"Terrific," said Mrs. Zachary.

Scritch went Stacy's chair.

Mrs. Zachary looked up. "Stacy, what are you doing?"

"Nothing." Stacy scritched back to her table.

Mrs. Zachary began to give out boxes. "Put your names on the bottom."

Jiwon got a pink one.

A.J. got a green one. "I can't do my name yet," he said.

Stacy reached over.

She put a big A.J. on his box.

Eddie got a green box.

Then Patty got the purple one. "Gorgeous," she said.

She jangled her bracelet.

Mrs. Zachary gave Stacy a tan one.

"Want to switch?" Stacy asked.

"Are you kidding?" Patty said.

"Stop jangling," Stacy said. "You're giving me a headache."

She banged the box over.

She wrote *S T A C Y A.* with her purple crayon.

Then she sat back.

It wasn't going to be such a hot week after all.

CHAPTER
2

"Playtime," said Mrs. Zachary.

Stacy sat up straight.

Straight as a stick.

Mrs. Zachary didn't see her, though. "A.J.," she said.

"I'll take the blocks," said A.J.

Good, thought Stacy.

Blocks weren't so hot.

Twana got the three-wheeler.

That wasn't so hot either.

"Two people for the little house," said Mrs. Zachary.

Stacy shot up. "Me."

"Me too," said her best friend Jiwon.

"And me," Patty said at the same time.

Stacy held up her fingers. "Only two," she told Patty.

She pointed to herself. "I'm one."

She pointed to Jiwon. "She's two."

Patty stuck out her lip.

They looked at Mrs. Zachary.

"Well," said Mrs. Zachary, "I guess it can be three this time."

"Yahoodie," said Patty.

They raced to the little house . . . into the almost-real kitchen.

They put the pots and pans on the almost-real stove.

"What can we cook?" Jiwon asked.

"Beans," said Patty.

"Yucks," Stacy said. She stopped to think. "I was in the jungle today. I shot a lion. We'll have him for supper."

"What about dessert?" Jiwon asked.

"No dessert," said Stacy. "I lost my money in the jungle. We have no cake."

"How do you make lion soup?" Jiwon asked.

"Easy. You put some soup in the pot. Then put in a cup of salt, a cup of pepper." Stacy raised her hands in the air. "And the lion."

"That's all?" Jiwon asked.

"Yes. Don't put in tomatoes. They make me shiver."

They both laughed.

Patty wasn't laughing, though. She kept rattling the pots. She

jangled her bracelet. "A lion is silly," she said.

Stacy frowned. "You make a lot of noise with that bracelet."

"It's my birthday bracelet," Patty said. "Remember? I got it at my party."

"No." Stacy shook her head.

Patty put her hand over her mouth. "I forgot. I didn't invite you."

Stacy made an I-don't-care face.

"Wait a minute," Patty said. "It was before school. I didn't know you then."

Stacy changed her I-don't-care face.

She made a friendly face.

They all laughed.

"What are you going to put in your About-Me box?" Jiwon asked.

"Wonderful stuff," said Patty. "The best."

"Mine is going to be the best too," said Stacy.

"I'm going to put in a little scrap of a dress," said Jiwon. "It's from when I was a baby. A little teeny pink lacy . . ."

Stacy nodded. "That's a great idea."

"I'm going to put in some special stuff," said Patty. "Special deluxe."

Jiwon hopped up a little. "What?"

Stacy wanted hers to be special deluxe too. "Want to hear about mine?" she asked.

She hoped she could think of something.

"In a minute," said Patty. "Me first."

"How come you're first?" Stacy asked.

Patty leaned closer.

She jangled her birthday bracelet.

The red heart on the end swung back and forth.

"You have a yucko box," she told Stacy.

"It's not so bad," said Jiwon.

"It's terrible," said Patty.

Stacy sucked in her lips.

She wanted to hit Patty right in her fat mouth.

"It can't be special deluxe," said Patty. "That's all."

Stacy stood up. She walked out of the house.

Then she went over to the girls'
room.

It was the little one . . . right in
the classroom.

Stacy took off the green GO sign.

She put up the red STOP sign.

She went inside and closed the
door.

Patty was right.

How could she be special with-
out a special box?

She had to do something about
it.

She had to do something fast.

CHAPTER
3

It was counting time.

Mrs. Zachary gave out chips.

Green ones and yellow ones. Orange ones and red ones.

Stacy had to put five orange ones in one pile.

Five green ones in another.

She was finished one-two-three.

She raised her hand.

Mrs. Zachary was busy at her desk. She didn't look at Stacy.

Stacy scritched her chair back and forth.

Mrs. Zachary looked up.

"Can I get a drink?" Stacy asked.

"May I," said Mrs. Zachary.

"May I," said Stacy.

Mrs. Zachary nodded. She began to work at her desk again.

Stacy waited a minute.

No one was looking.

She took her box.

She walked out of the room.

It was fun to walk around the school.

She walked fast.

She clicked her feet hard.

Then she stopped.

Suppose the principal came along? Mr. Mancina.

He'd know she was going to do something terrible.

He'd know she was going to get rid of that tan box.

The ugliest box in the world.

Stacy saw the auditorium doors.

Quickly she opened them a crack.

A fifth grader was taking his drum lesson.

He was banging the drum like crazy.

He was crashing pot-cover things together.

Stacy would love to crash them too.

"Very good," said the music teacher.

The boy stood up.

Stacy closed the doors again.

She bent down.

She took a quick drink.

The water was cold. Too cold.

It made her lips feel numb.

The boy and the teacher came out. They went up the stairs.

Stacy raced into the auditorium.
The doors closed behind her.
She had never been in here alone before.
Suppose someone came in?
She started down the aisle.
She looked back.
No one was coming.
She could see the drums on the stage.
Next to them was a table.
It had a gold skirt around it.
On top were those round crash-ing pot-cover things.
She'd never touch them.
Of course not.

She didn't touch other people's property.

She was just going to have a little look.

She went across the front.

Up the steps.

There they were . . . all gold and silver and wood.

Gorgeous.

She was sick of carrying the tan box. She'd put it down for a minute.

What would happen if she picked up those crashing things?

Nothing.

The boy wouldn't care.

They were supposed to be crashed.

She reached out to touch one.

It was shiny. Neat. Heavier than she had thought.

She gave it a flick with one finger.

Plink.

She put her hand in the straps.

Then she picked them both up.

"I am the drummer," she sang. "Drum drum, drummer."

She gave them a little crash.

Nobody could even hear them.

She could hardly hear them herself.

She was dying to give them a
big fat crash.

What would Mrs. Zachary say?

She thought for a moment.

Mrs. Zachary would say it was
the auditorium. It was perfectly
all right to make music noise in
there.

Stacy looked at the doors . . .
just in case.

They were closed tight.

She held the crashing things far
apart.

Then she rammed them together.
BANG!
"Wooie," she told herself.
She was dying to take drum lessons.
Too bad it would take forever to get to fifth grade.
She held them apart again.
BANG! BANG!
Special deluxe.
Just then the auditorium doors opened.
Stacy's heart began to pound.
She could feel it thumping.
It sounded like drums.

She grabbed the box.

She slid underneath the table.

The sweeper man was out there. Jim.

She hoped he didn't take too long.

It was hot under the table.

She wiggled around a little.

She sat back on something hard.

"Ouch," she said.

Jim didn't hear her. He began to sing. "Giddyap horsie, I'm goin' to ride. . . ."

Even Eddie could sing better than that. And Eddie was the worst singer in the class.

Stacy scrunched her head down.
She laughed into her shirt.
After a while she stopped.
She peeked out.

Jim was going to be there forever.

What was Mrs. Zachary going
to say?

Just then the door opened.

"Can you give me a minute?"
Mr. Mancina asked.

"Sure thing," said Jim.

The door slammed shut behind
him.

Stacy crawled out.

She felt around for the box.

She had sat on it.

"Squasho," she said.

That was the end of the ugliest box in the world.

She shoved it under the table again.

She raced back to the room.

"That was a long drink of water," Mrs. Zachary said.

Stacy ducked her head.

She walked back to her seat with her eyes down.

CHAPTER

4

It was getting dark.

Stacy lay on the floor in her living room.

Cartoons were on.

Emily was on the floor too. She had to do homework.

She kept erasing.

Stacy tapped her shoulder. "Suppose someone comes in the window."

Emily shook her head. "Don't be dumb."

"Oh, yes, Emily," said Stacy. "It's a monster with a gold tail. He has a tongue with fire."

Their mother came into the living room. "No wonder you can't do that," she told Emily. "Sit at the kitchen table."

Emily banged into the kitchen.

Stacy stayed in the living room. She watched a zillion cartoons.

Then she remembered.

"Do we have any boxes?" she yelled to her mother.

Her mother didn't answer.

Stacy stood up. She went into the kitchen.

Emily was at the table.

Her face was red.

"I hate subtraction," she said.

"Me too," said Stacy.

Emily laughed. "You don't know what subtraction is."

"No," said Stacy. "I hate it anyway."

She pulled at her mother's sweater. "Do we have any boxes?"

"In the attic," said her mother.

"I need one."

"I'm busy," said her mother. "Making stew."

"Does it have those tomatoes sliding around?"

"Sure," said her mother.

"They give me a stomachache."

"No, they don't." Her mother tasted the stew with the big spoon. "Oo la la," she said. "Wonderful."

She swooped down.

She gave Stacy a hug.

"I need a box," Stacy said. "Right this minute. I have to take it to school tomorrow."

Her mother sighed. "Let me finish here."

"I need—" Stacy began.

Her mother picked up the big spoon. "This spoon can be used for a lot of things."

Stacy dashed out of the kitchen. "You can't catch me."

Her mother laughed.

She kept cooking.

Stacy went into the living room.

The worst cartoon in the world was on.

Maybe she should get the box herself.

Yes. That's just what she'd do.

She went upstairs.

She opened the attic door.

It was dark.

She put on the light.

"Anyone here?" she yelled. "I'm coming with that big spoon. I'm going to bash you over the head."

She listened.

Nobody was scritchy-scratching around up there.

It was probably safe.

She went up the stairs slowly
. . . just in case.

If she heard a noise, she'd run.

She'd run like a tiger.

It was cold up there.

Very cold.

She looked around.

Boxes and books and pictures
were all over the place.

An old mirror stood in the corner.

Clothes were piled on a baby carriage. Her mother's long red gown.
Emily's first-day-of-school dress.

She took a look at some of the
boxes.

Which one should she choose?

It had to be special deluxe . . . better than old jingle-jangle Patty's.

She saw a gold one in the corner.

Gorgeous.

It was going to be hard to get, though.

A zillion things were piled in front of it.

She stepped over a jacket.

She put one foot on the checkers game-board.

Her other foot landed on a lampshade.

The gold box was just a little farther away.

She leaned over.

She reached out . . . and pulled at the edge of the box.

A few other boxes toppled over. Then it was free.

"Got it," she sang. "Got, got, got it." She pulled it toward her.

It was light. Light as a feather.

She opened it.

It was filled with Christmas-tree ornaments.

Red ones, green ones, little silvery icicles.

She'd have to put them some-where.

There was room behind the mirror.

Carefully she dumped them out.

Some of them rolled around a little.

That was all right.

They didn't roll far.

Stacy stopped to look in the mirror.

There she was.

Tan hair.

Tan eyes.

Almost no eyebrows.

She looked closer.

She looked like a camel, she thought.

She wasn't special deluxe.

She wasn't even special.

Her About-Me box couldn't be special either.

CHAPTER

5

Outside the school it was snowing.

Inside, Stacy was cutting out a snowflake.

She couldn't think of anything else to do.

"That's not about you," Patty said. She leaned closer. "Hey. That's not your box."

Stacy pulled the gold box closer. "It is so."

"You had a tan one," said Patty. "A stinky tan one." Her hand shot up. "Mrs. Zachary," she yelled.

"Be quiet." Stacy reached out. She pulled Patty's arm down.

"Ouch," Patty said.

"Big baby," Stacy said. "It didn't even hurt."

Mrs. Zachary looked up. "What's going on?"

"It's about Stacy's box," said Patty.

"Worry about your own box," said Mrs. Zachary.

"Yes," said Stacy. "Worry about your own stinky box."

She said it in a small voice.

She didn't want anyone to hear.

"I think Stacy's saying bad words," Patty said.

"That's enough," said Mrs. Zachary. "I want you both to get down to work."

Stacy turned around.

She didn't want to look at Patty.

She crumpled up the snowflake. She sailed it into the wastepaper basket.

She couldn't think of one About-Me thing.

If only she weren't a camel.

If only she were special deluxe.

She picked up a magazine. She started to look through it.

"Look," Patty told Jiwon.

Stacy looked over her shoulder.

Patty was holding up her drawing.

It was a girl in a long pink dress.

"Gorgeous, right?" Patty said. "It's me. I was a flower girl."

"You look like a weed girl," Stacy said.

She wanted to cry.

Nobody had asked her to be a flower girl.

She couldn't blame them.

Who wanted a camel walking down the aisle?

She turned to another page.

It was a picture of a girl in a red dress.

It had diamonds all over it.

Better than Patty's.

Much.

She'd cut it out. Stick it in her About-Me box. *I was a flower girl, too,* she'd say.

On the next page was a bracelet.

It was gold and red and green.

Sparkly.

"It's my birthday bracelet," she'd say. *"Before I came to school."*

She picked up her scissors.

She began to cut.

Just then Mrs. Zachary stood up. She went to the front. "Everyone's working hard," she said. "This is the best class."

"Better than Emily's?" Stacy asked.

"Emily's class was nice too," said Mrs. Zachary. She clapped her hands. "I have a great surprise."

Everyone sat up straight.

"Tomorrow your parents can

come," Mrs. Zachary said. "They can see the About-Me boxes."

"How about my aunt?" A.J. asked.

"Lovely," said Mrs. Zachary.

Stacy stopped cutting.

She put down her scissors.

Her mother knew she hadn't been a flower girl.

She knew Stacy didn't have a red dress with diamonds . . . or a sparkly bracelet.

Stacy sailed the pictures into the basket.

They landed on top of the snow-flake.

Then the door opened.

Stacy looked up.

It was the fifth-grade boy. The one who took drum lessons.

He had a tan box in his hand.

It was a mess.

Squasho.

Stacy ducked behind Jiwon.

"Is Stacy A. in this class?" he asked.

Patty stood up.

She pointed her finger at Stacy.

Stacy shook her head hard.

"It must be another Stacy A.," she said.

CHAPTER
6

Everyone was gone.

Almost everyone.

Mr. Bell had come to get the class.

It was time for recess.

Stacy was still there, though. And so was Mrs. Zachary.

The squasho box was on the table.

Mrs. Zachary wanted to talk with Stacy.

Stacy could feel her heart beating.

She drew an *S* on her thumb.

Then she drew an *A*.

Mrs. Zachary sat down with her.

Stacy didn't look up.

"When are you going to tell me?" she asked.

"Tell you what?" Stacy made a face on her wrist.

It was a frowning face.

Her heart was beating fast.

Mrs. Zachary put her hand over Stacy's.

Stacy waited a little. "You mean about the box?"

"Exactly," said Mrs. Zachary.

"I hate that box."

"Why didn't you tell me that? I might have found another one."

"I never thought of it," Stacy said.

"Besides," said Mrs. Zachary, "it's what's in the box that counts."

Stacy didn't say anything.

She started another face.

A sad face.

"I won't do it again," she told Mrs. Zachary.

Mrs. Zachary patted her arm. "Next time don't hide things. And don't go anywhere unless I know about it."

"Never," said Stacy. She shook her head. "I don't like to be in trouble."

Mrs. Zachary nodded. "You're a great girl, Stacy."

"Not special deluxe, though."

"Everyone is special deluxe," said Mrs. Zachary.

She smiled with her big teeth.

Stacy smiled back.

She made her teeth stick out too.

Then she sighed. Mrs. Zachary didn't understand.

There wasn't one special deluxe thing about her.

"Hurry now," said Mrs. Zachary. "Don't miss recess."

Stacy yanked her hat over her head.

She took her jacket.

She went down the hall.

Outside it was cold.

Stacy opened her mouth.

The wind pulled her breath away.

She caught up with Jiwon.

Jiwon began to run.

Stacy ran too.

She held out her arms. "The wind is coming," she yelled. "It's going to take us."

Patty came after them.

Then A.J.

"Hurry," Stacy yelled. "It's going to drop us off the world."

"Yeow," yelled Jiwon. "It will take the About-Me boxes."

Stacy stopped running.

She thought about tomorrow.

She thought about the mothers and fathers coming.

There was nothing in her About-Me box.

Not one thing.

She sighed. "I don't want to play anymore."

"What's the end of the story?" Jiwon asked.

"I don't know," Stacy said.

She raised her shoulders up.

She felt like crying.

"You have to make it up yourself," she said.

"I don't know how," said Jiwon.

Just then Mr. Bell blew his whistle.

"It's time to go in anyway," said
Patty.

The class lined up.

They started up the stairs.

Then Stacy thought of something.

She stopped.

Something special?

Something special deluxe?

Maybe, she thought.

She'd have to hurry.

She didn't have much time.

CHAPTER
7

It was Thursday.

Everyone would be there soon.

Stacy was drawing.

Crayons were all over the table.

Fat yellow ones. Green. Dark purple.

Up in front Mrs. Zachary was putting cookies on a plate.

"I'm dying for one," Eddie told Stacy.

"Me too," said Stacy.

"Too bad we have to wait," he said.

Stacy picked up a purple crayon.

She started her last picture.

Then the door opened.

It was A.J.'s father.

Jiwon's mother came next. Then Eddie's father.

Stacy drew as fast as she could.

The door opened again.

It was her mother.

And a surprise.

Her Nana Rosie was there too.

Stacy was glad she had on her new shirt.

It had teddy bears all over it.
She stood up for a minute.
She wanted Nana to see it.
Nana waved. So did her mother.
Stacy slapped her paper into her box.
She was ready.
She sat up so Mrs. Zachary could see.
Mrs. Zachary smiled at everyone. "I think it's time to begin."
"Me too," said Eddie.
"Would you like to be first?" Mrs. Zachary asked him.
Eddie raced to the front.

His box was filled with food pictures. Ice cream and peaches. A candy bar and an apple.

"I used to have a real potato chip," he said. "Only a little is left."

He held it up. He popped it into his mouth.

Everyone laughed.

Eddie's father laughed the hardest. "Good boy," he said.

Mrs. Zachary looked around. "How about . . ."

Everyone sat up straight.

Straight as sticks.

"Patty," said Mrs. Zachary.

Patty raced up to the front.

She held up her flower-girl picture.

Stacy was getting sick of looking at it.

Patty's mother was smiling.

She took out a camera.

She took Patty's picture.

Stacy looked out the window.

Maybe Patty's mother thought she was special.

Special deluxe.

Stacy snorted.

Patty held up a picture. Three sticks holding hands.

"These are my best friends," she said.

Stacy made an I-don't-care face.

"Jiwon, Twana, and Stacy," said Patty.

Stacy felt her face change.

She smiled at Patty.

Patty wasn't so bad after all.

Twana was next.

She had a picture of a black dog.

He had a smushed-in face.

He had one tooth that stuck out.

"This is Beauty," said Twana. "He's the best."

Beauty was a mess, Stacy thought. She wanted to laugh.

She didn't, though.

She didn't want to hurt Twana's feelings.

Other people took their turns.

Jiwon, and A.J., and Carter.

Stacy was sick of waiting.

She leaned on the table . . . and something else.

It was the gold box.

Squasho.

"Your turn, Stacy," said Mrs. Zachary.

Stacy went to the front.

Everyone was looking at her.

Her mother . . . Nana Rosie . . . the other mothers and fathers.

Stacy held up the squasho box.
Nobody looked at it.
They were smiling at her.
"My best thing is this," she said.
"I like to tell stories."

She held up a picture of a monster. "He has a tail and gold eyes. I told Emily about it."

Next she held up a cutout. It was a girl. She was crying.

"That's the story of the lost girl," said Jiwon. "The one in the snow."

"Yes," said Stacy. She held up a purple picture.

"This is the wind whooshing around."

She raised her shoulders. "I didn't finish this yet."

Stacy took a breath. "This last picture has a drum. It has me playing the crashing things. It's a birthday story."

She looked at her mother.

"For my next birthday."

Everybody laughed.

A nice laugh.

Stacy laughed too.

Mrs. Zachary stood up. "The children worked hard."

"Right," said Patty.

"They're special," said Mrs. Zachary. "Special because they're friends, special because we love them."

Stacy looked up.

"Hey, that's right," she said.

Patty was jangling her bracelet again.

She looked at Stacy and smiled.

Then Eddie's father began to clap.

So did the other mothers and fathers.

Stacy clapped too.

Then she raced to the front.

She wanted to be first for a cookie.